Especially for
With love from

For Brent, Angela and Eric, my precious children
whom God has given me to pray for and love—B.K.

To all the angels in my life, both seen and unseen—N.B.

As I Kneel
Published By WaterBrook Press
5446 North Academy Boulevard, Suite 200
Colorado Springs, Colorado 80908
A division of Bantam Doubleday Dell Publishing Group, Inc

Mops (Mothers of Preschoolers) is a program designed
for mothers with children under school age.
For more information call or write:
Mops International, P.O. Box 102200
Denver, CO 80250-2200
303-733-5353 E-mail: Info@MOPS.org

Published in association with the literary agency
of Alive Communications, Inc.,
1465 Kelly Johnson Blvd. Suite 320
Colorado Springs, CO 80920

ISBN 1-57856-025-X

Printed in the United States of America
June 1998—First Edition

1 3 5 7 9 10 8 6 4 2

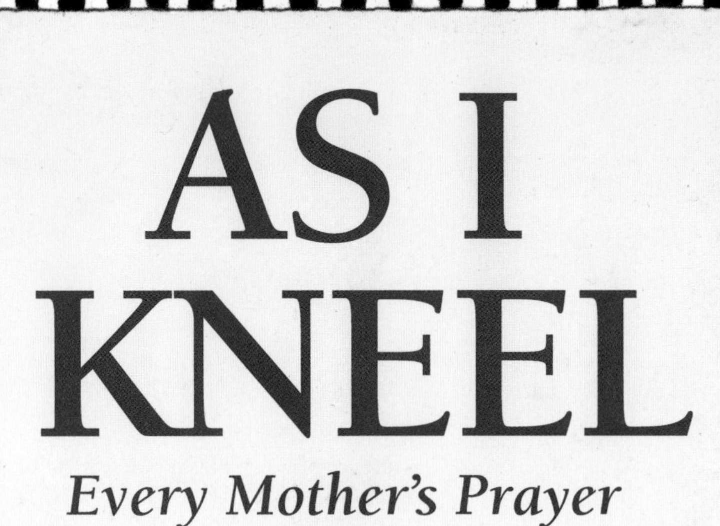

AS I KNEEL

Every Mother's Prayer

BY BONNIE KNOPF
ILLUSTRATED BY NAN BROOKS

WATERBROOK
PRESS

And all the angel
Hear mother'
Day and night I say
Lord, keep

everywhere ...
love as it fills the air
this quiet prayer
my child in your care

As I kneel beside your bed tonight,

I pray that God's love
holds you tight.

And keeps you safe
'til morning's light,

As I kneel beside your bed tonight.

And all the angel
Hear mother'
Day and night I sa
Lord, keep

everywhere ...
love as it fills the air
this quiet prayer
my child in your care

In the park,
I watch you run,

Blowing bubbles in the sun.

Swinging, climbing,
having fun!

How I love you, little one!

And all the angel
Hear mother'
Day and night I say
Lord, keep

everywhere ...
love as it fills the air
this quiet prayer
my child in your care

STOP

The school bus comes,
we kiss good-bye

Where did all your baby years fly?

As I pray for you
the whole day through

I know God's love is
surrounding you!

And all the angels
Hear mother's
Day and night I say
Lord, keep

everywhere ...
love as it fills the air
this quiet prayer
my child in your care

1
10K
BHS

I blink my eyes,
and you're a teen,

With music, friends
and magazines.

When times are tough,
I pray you'll see,

You're loved by God,
you're loved by me!

And all the angel
Hear mother'
Day and night I say
Lord, keep

everywhere ...
love as it fills the air
his quiet prayer
ny child in your care

Packing your bags and leaving home,
Driving away, you're on your own.
I'm still your mom, but more your friend.
You know my prayers will never end.

And all the angel
Hear mother'
Day and night I say
Lord, keep

everywhere ...
love as it fills the air
this quiet prayer
my child in your care

You will hold
your child someday

And then your love will light the way,
I'll kneel beside you while we pray

And bless the child
God sent our way.

And all the angel
Hear mother'
Day and night I say
Lord, keep

everywhere ...
love as it fills the air
this quiet prayer
my child in your care

Thank you, Mom, for showing me
How great a mother's love can be.
You showed how much you cared for me
By praying for me endlessly.

And all the angel
Hear mother'
Day and night I say
Lord, keep

everywhere ...
love as it fills the air
this quiet prayer
my child in your care

Now I'm the one to kneel tonight,
As all the stars are shining bright.
I pray that God will hold you tight

And keep you safe 'til morning's light.

And all the angels
everywhere
Hear a child's love
fill the air.
Day and night
we say this quiet prayer,
Lord keep us all
in your perfect care
All over the world, yes,
EVERYWHERE!